# I Can Read...

# Cinderella

Once upon a time, there was a
beautiful, kind girl called Cinderella.
She lived with her stepmother and
two stepsisters.
They were not kind to Cinderella.
She had to cook and clean all day.
Cinderella did all the work.

This igloo book belongs to:

. . . . . . . . . . . . . . . . . . . . . . .

. . . . . . . . . . . . . . . . . . . . . . .

# Reading Together

This story is written in a special way so that a child and an adult can 'take turns' in reading the text.

The left-hand side is for the adult to read.

Cinderella's fairy godmother waved her magic wand.

Cinderella's fairy godmother waved her magic wand.
The pumpkin turned into a golden coach.
The mice turned into four white horses.
And the cat turned into a coachman.

The right-hand side has a simple sentence (taken from the story) which the child reads.

Firstly, it is always helpful to read the whole book to your child, stopping to talk about the pictures. Explain that you are going to read it again but this time the child can join in.

Read the left-hand page and when you come to the sentence which is repeated on the other page run your finger under it. Your child then tries to read the same sentence opposite.

Searching for the child's sentence in the adult version is a useful activity. Your child will have a real sense of achievement when all the sentences on the right-hand page can be read. Giving lots of praise is very important.

**Enjoy the story together.**

Cinderella did all the work.

One day, a letter came from the palace.
The prince was having a ball.
"You have to stay at home," her
stepmother and stepsisters told
Cinderella. She had to help them put on
their best dresses.

The prince was having a ball.

Cinderella was very sad.
She was sitting alone by the fire when
a beautiful woman appeared.
"I am your fairy godmother," she said.
"You shall go to the ball! Bring me a
pumpkin, four mice and a cat."

# Cinderella was very sad.

Cinderella's fairy godmother waved her magic wand.
The pumpkin turned into a golden coach.
The mice turned into four white horses.
And the cat turned into a coachman.

Cinderella's fairy godmother
waved her magic wand.

"I cannot go to the ball in my old clothes,"
said Cinderella.

Her fairy godmother waved her wand
again. Now Cinderella wore a beautiful
dress and glass slippers.

"Enjoy yourself at the ball," she told
Cinderella. "But remember − you have to
be home by midnight."

Cinderella wore a beautiful dress
and glass slippers.

Cinderella was the most beautiful girl
at the ball. She danced with Prince
Charming all night.
She did not notice the time.
Then the clock struck twelve!
Quickly, Cinderella ran down the stairs
to her coach.

Then the clock struck twelve!

Cinderella ran so fast that one of her
slippers fell off.
The prince ran after her. He did not
see Cinderella, but the Prince found
Cinderella's slipper.
"I will marry the girl who can wear this
slipper," he said.

The prince found Cinderella's slipper.

The prince looked everywhere for the
girl who could wear the glass slipper.
At last, he came to Cinderella's house.
One of her stepsisters tried to put on the
slipper. It was too small.
"Ouch!" she cried.
Cinderella's other stepsister tried to put
on the slipper.
It was too small for her, too.
The slipper did not fit the stepsisters.

# The slipper did not fit the stepsisters.

"Please, may I try on the slipper?"
asked Cinderella.
"Don't be silly," said her stepmother.
But the prince let Cinderella try on the
glass slipper.
It fitted Cinderella perfectly.

It fitted Cinderella perfectly.

Prince Charming and Cinderella fell in love.
Cinderella forgave her stepsisters and
made them promise to be kind to
everyone. They all lived happily ever after.

Prince Charming and
Cinderella fell in love.

# Key Words

Can you read these words and find them in the book?

fairy godmother

stepsisters

glass slipper

Cinderella

coach

# Questions and Answers

Now that you've read the story can you answer these questions?

a. Who did all the work?

b. What did the mice turn into?

c. Who found Cinderella's slipper?

a. Cinderella  b. White horses  c. The prince

# Tell your own Story

Can you make up a different story
with the pictures and words below?

**coach and horses**

**palace**

magic wand

clock

stepmother

mice

slipper

beautiful girl

prince

# Mix and Match

Draw a line from the pictures to the correct word to match them up.

clock

prince

slipper

Cinderella

pumpkin

mice